Suggestions for Parents

First, read the book to your child. Allow him or her all the time needed to look closely at the pictures and to discuss the story. Then—even on another day—read the story again, now pointing to the words as you read them. After a few readings, the child who is ready to read will begin to pick up the often-repeated words—even the big ones! Before long (there's no hurry) the child will try to read the book alone. It is most important that you patiently build your child's confidence and give him or her the sense that reading is fun. You will find that there is nothing to match the excitement and satisfaction your child will feel on learning to read *a whole book*!

Tunafish Sandwiches

By Patty Wolcott
Illustrated by Hans Zander

Random House 🏠 New York

Library of Congress Cataloging-in-Publication Data:
Wolcott, Patty.
    Tunafish sandwiches / by Patty Wolcott ; illustrated by Hans
Zander.
        p. cm. — (Ten-word readers)
    Originally published: Reading, Mass. : Addison-Wesley, 1975.
    Summary: Pictures and brief text introduce the concept of a food
chain, beginning with the part tiny phytoplankton play in providing
tuna for two children's tunafish sandwiches.
    ISBN 0-679-81927-4 (trade) — ISBN 0-679-91927-9 (lib. bdg.)
    1. Food chains (Ecology)—Juvenile literature. 2. Marine ecology—
Juvenile literature. [1. Food chains (Ecology) 2. Marine
ecology. 3. Ecology.]   I. Zander, Hans, 1937– ill.   II. Title.
III. Series: Wolcott, Patty. Ten-word readers.
QH541.14.W64   1991
574.5′3—dc20   91-13496

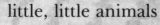

little, little plants   little, little animals

 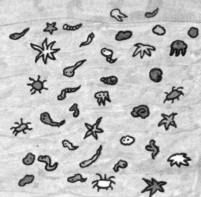

Little, little animals eat little, little plants.

little, little plants   little, little animals

little fish

little, little animals

little,
little plants

little fish

Little fish eat
little, little animals.

little fish

big fish

little fish

Big fish eat little fish.

big fish

big fish

BIG, BIG fish

big fish

BIG, BIG fish eat big fish.

BIG, BIG fish

People eat BIG, BIG fish.

10-Word Readers
by Patty Wolcott

Double-Decker Double-Decker Double-Decker Bus
Eeeeeek!
The Marvelous Mud Washing Machine
Pickle Pickle Pickle Juice
Tunafish Sandwiches
Where Did That Naughty Little Hamster Go?